FAREWELL, CLAW!

Singspiel in two acts

NARRATOR

CLAW

SASTRAPOLUS
THE MASTER

THE MESSENGER
OF PALORIUS

INGRIDIUS

A MAN CARRYING
A STUMP

THE SPRING

MICHAEL THE TEEN

CAPTAIN
ODOBENUS

ANOTHER TEEN

ACT ONE

SCENE ONE

NARRATOR

The brass bells of the Nerovictus Academy toll
for the newly graduated.
Claw, a painter fresh out of school,
stood in the yard amid the celebrated:
Principal Proterius gave him a stipend
with his very own hand.
After the festivities,
Claw plodded through the hallways of the Academy
bidding farewell to fond memories.

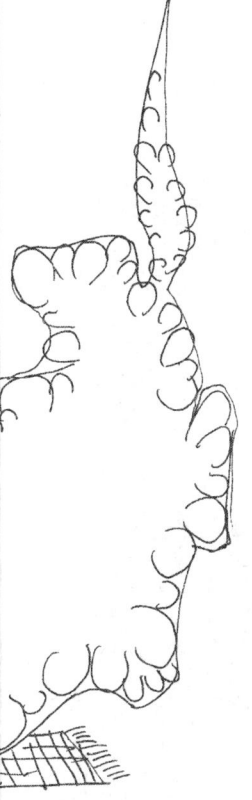

CLAW

In that auditorium,
a sack of gypsum fell, squashing a model,
and in this one,
the teacher of carpentry, Munrustus,
taught us to feel the wood,
and under these columns,
in front of Master Vectovius,
he sullied himself with a piece of chalk.
O the glory of it!

Let me ride to my hometown
and sing its glory:

This is how the folk of the village sing
when they see the artist revenant!

War, famine, plague, and demise!
On a birch leaf,
the ladybird catches an aphid!

Falsehood, debauchery, and weakness!
Remove the rotten tooth with pincers!

Mousebirds, hornbills and woodpeckers !
The brush conjures wonders!

This is how the folk of the village sang
when they saw the artist revenant.

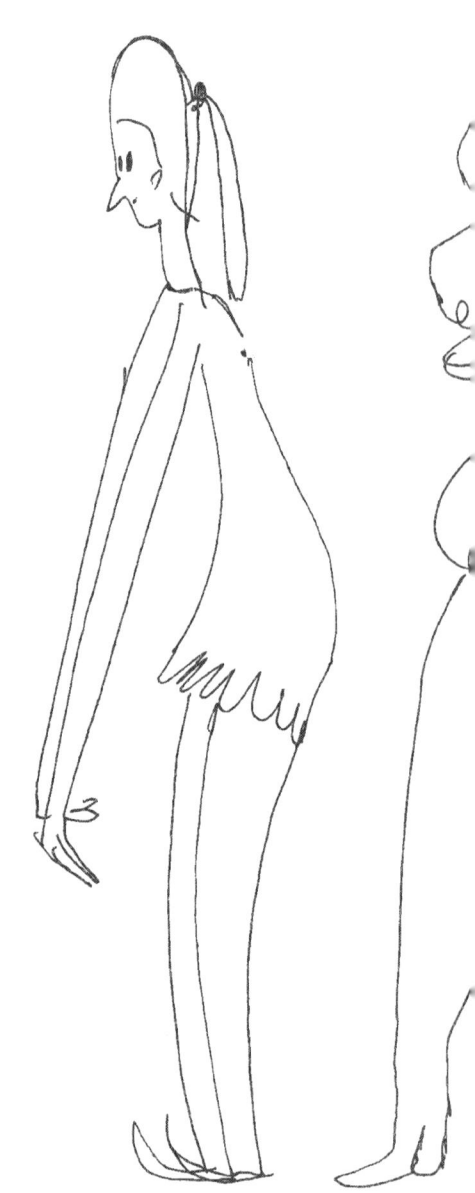

NARRATOR

Singing,
Claw walked through the town gates
and arrived at the old oak in due turn,
greeting it thus:

CLAW

O glory, at home at last!
That's the same oak,
the palette,
my childhood brushes,
the blueish gray à la El Greco,
form hard and soft
—they all now obey the eye of my hand.

Now I remember!
My old master,
Sastrapolus, lives nigh.
He taught me the 101 of art.
I'll paint him
and exhibit my newly acquired skills!
The plane has found
an old beard to smoothen!

SCENE TWO

NARRATOR

Claw arrived at the door of Sastrapolus the master and knocked thrice.

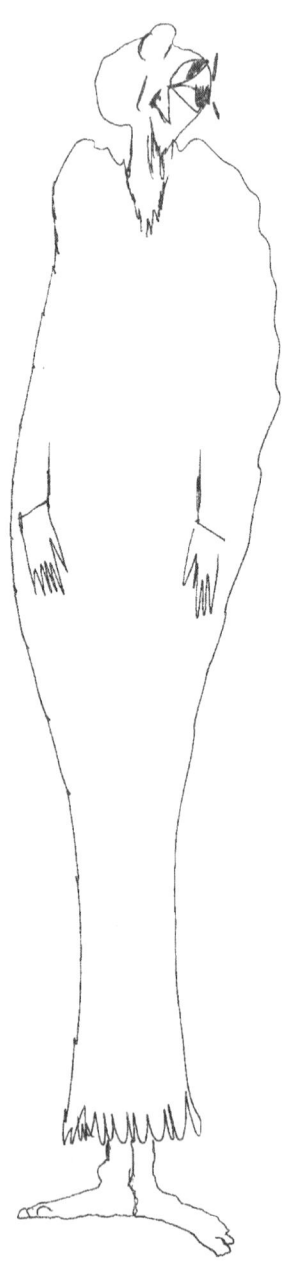

SASTRAPOLUS

Someone is about to penetrate my house!
O figure, reveal your form!

CLAW

'Tis me, Claw!

SASTRAPOLUS

I've never heard of a fellow with such a name!

CLAW

What, you don't remember your old student?
Have you forgotten
who attached your charcoal to its place?
Who skinned the pine marten
and boiled the glue out of the rabbit?

SASTRAPOLUS

Ah, I know you!
It's you—Claw!
What's your business in these parts?

CLAW

I intend to paint you!
I know the light, the line!
The lie, the error, the truth!

SASTRAPOLUS

Whence such certainty?
Perchance your eye lies about beauty,
your hand does not follow the mind?

CLAW

I'm as certain as one can be,
for genius raises its head in my works.
That head is my bedrock,
from where I dive into a pond,
quenching my thirst with its liquid brightness!

SASTRAPOLUS

You talk lovely of yourself,
but beware the snare of hubris!
Kneel and stick your hands into the soil,
letting the seedling sprout.
Water it and caress it,
carry it with yourself always.

CLAW

You are a sage, a gardener of art!
I don't care about seedlings, however,
I'm already a noble pine!
As for you, the leaves are falling off your tree,
turning you into a pallid being!

(Claw walks to the master and grabs his hand.)

SASTRAPOLUS

You're too late, there's no time to paint me.
My light is waning.
Darkness is coming,
and with it, death.
I won't get more time,
but rest, that my hand will get.
I'll solidify
like an old portrait.

CLAW

Your finger so stiff and cold,
I can feel your spirit fleeting!

SASTRAPOLUS

Your finger is still warm.
Laugh, run, play!
Believe in the truth of art!
Remember my words!

(Sastrapolus the master breaths his last.)

SCENE THREE

NARRATOR

And so Claw left the house of his old master,
intending to leave the town.
He journeyed the road,
looking for a topic for his painting.
He was filled with a sudden joie de vivre
and composed a new song.

KYNSI

I am journeying the road of art,
not picking a poisonous mushroom
but the wisdom of ancient moss.
I'll capture the spirit of the landscape.

I'll quench my thirst in the spring of art,
even the knight of Greatius
will bow in front of me.

(Claw stops his singing
when he sees Ingridius on the side of the road.)

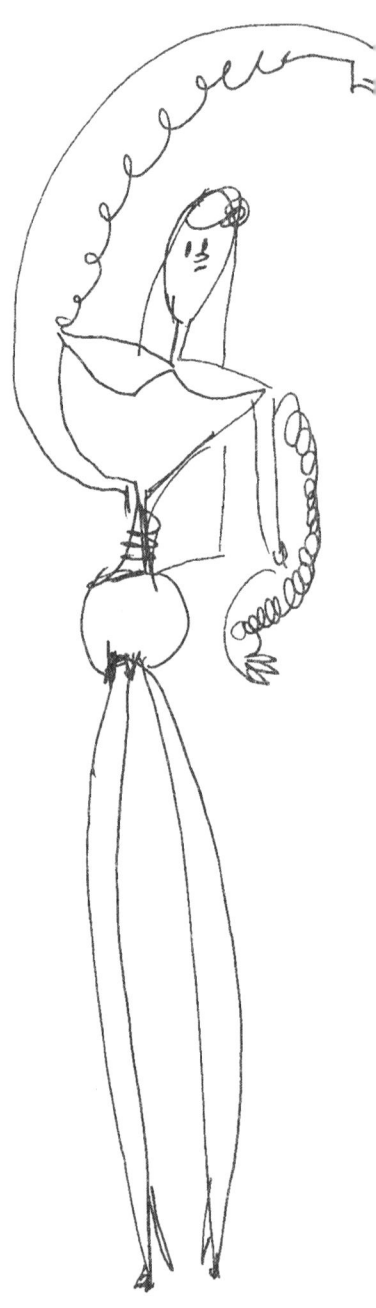

CLAW

O the symmetry! Who are you?
Can I preserve you on my canvas?

INGRIDIUS

Thank you for your kind words!
Ingridius is my name. You can paint me,
but tears run in my veins.
Can your brush see the unseen?

CLAW

I'll rise to the challenge!
When I'm finished with you,
your fragile soul will glow on the canvas!

(Ingridius sits on a stump.
Claw starts to paint.)

I N G R I D I U S

My father was a mystic,
the people feared him.
Mother was known for her beauty,
a light shone through her.
She loved the night.

Everyone made fun of me since I was little,
dogs barked, and Jo the Goose cackled.
And I was only getting medicine
for my father's gout.

My body made people at the village
feel insecure and afraid,
so I left when the Moon
had passed Taurus six times.

I was looking for my place in the world,
till I found myself under the copper roofs
of Raudos, in peace.

I don't hear jeers, nor do I see them.
So have I lived, so have I lived.

(Claw finishes painting.)

CLAW

Come see, the painting is ready!
I captured your spirit in it!

INGRIDIUS

You have mastered the cold and warm alla prima,
but I don't see my soul in it.

CLAW

You cheap piece of grass!
This is a piece of mastery!

INGRIDIUS

You looked at me through the bug-eyed eyes
of Jo the Goose,
thinning your paint with rabies dribble.
You are one of those who jeer.

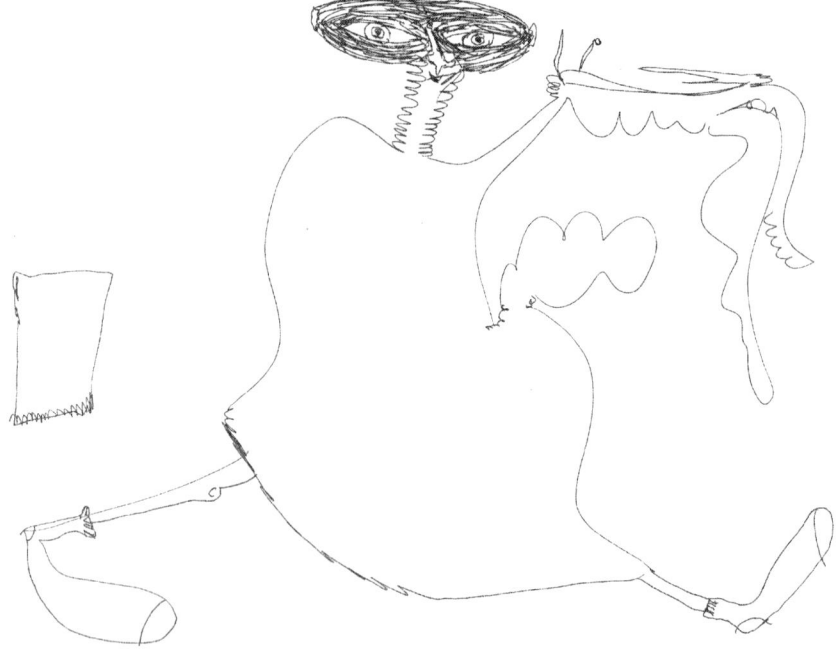

CLAW

Phew!
In my pouch made of pig bladder I have a stipend,
given to me by Principal Proterius
with his very own hand.
I'm walking the road of beauty in monk strap shoes!

INGRIDIUS

You are walking the road of evil,
not knowing love.
You see yourself everywhere.
In your hands, a rose becomes mere thorns.

(Exit Ingridius.
Claw is left alone with his painting.)

SCENE FOUR

NARRATOR

The wind gained in strength,
the sky became dark,
John the Rabbit cried from behind the bush.
At that moment, Claw noticed something
approaching from the sky
and descending in front of him.

CLAW

Am I being struck by the lightning
of the god Tars
or the Reaper of Geaus?
Who are you?

THE MESSENGER OF PALORIUS

I am the Messenger of Palorius.
I observe the time, see the direction,
and master absolute speed.

CLAW

Your reputation precedes you,
O Messenger!
The inhabitants of the Earth
have heard rumors about you.
Did you come to admire
my painting?

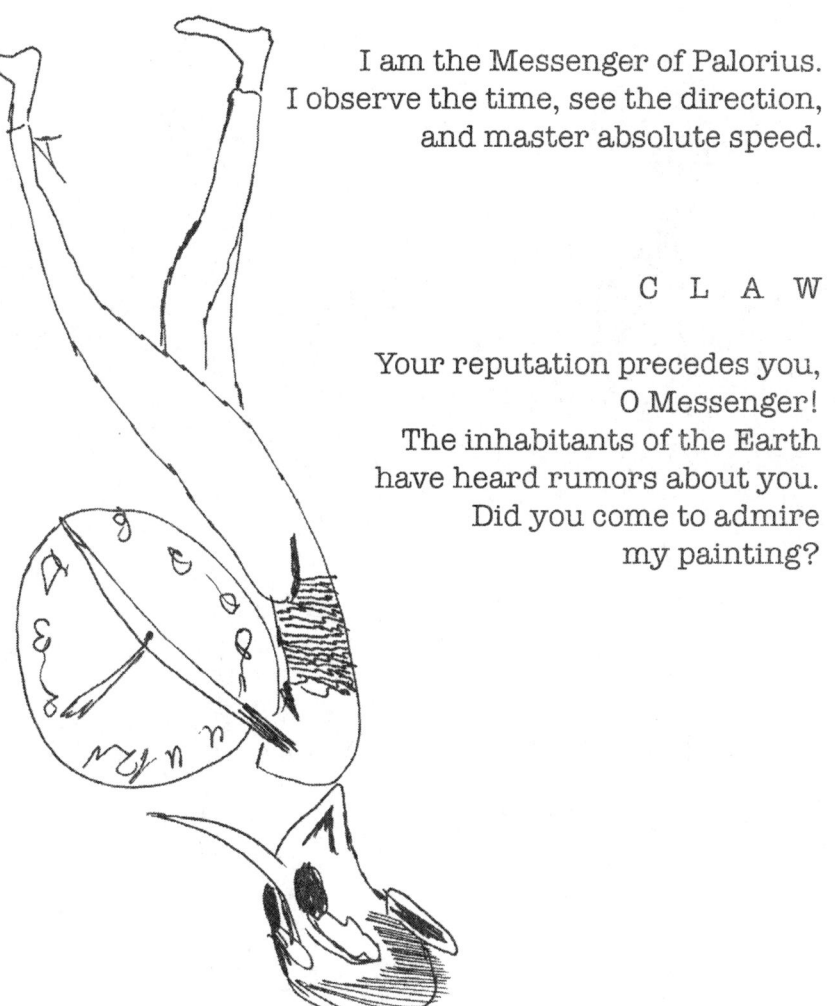

(The Messenger of Palorious regards the painting.)

THE MESSENGER OF PALORIUS

Everything is superficially in order,
yet I cannot but deem this slavish emulation.
The shrew is climbing along the edge of the eaves.

CLAW

You who observe the time,
your words are like daggers!
Is my work utterly worthless?

THE MESSENGER OF PALORIUS

Everything has some value,
it's not easy to produce thought.
Even Morris the Otter of the Waterworld
drowns at times.

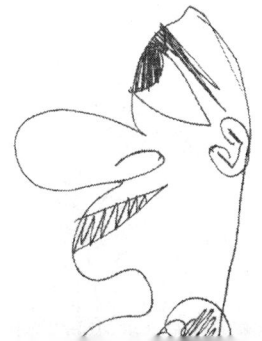

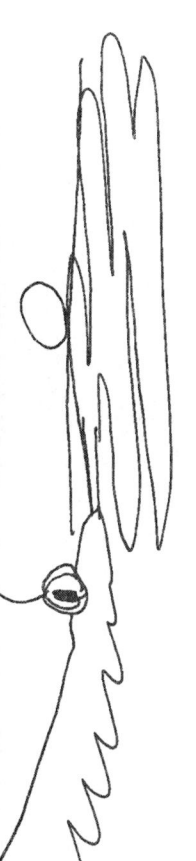

CLAW

It's a rat that drowns.
An otter stays afloat, diving only for fish!
Our time might have flaws
but nature is timeless!
Hence, it contains the essence
of everything!
My hand will grasp the ungraspable!
Mark my words, O wise Messenger!

THE MESSENGER
OF PALORIUS

As you wish,
I will allow you the opportunity.
When the constellation of Vicovarius
shines bright in the morning,
I will appear to you.
You shall present me your new painting
then and there.

(The Messenger of Palorious disappears.)

SCENE FIVE

NARRATOR

Once again Claw journeyed the road,
looking for a comely landscape,
perhaps a crooked tree.
When he came to Coltsfoot,
a man arose from under a stump
and cried out irritated:

A MAN CARRYING A STUMP

> Out of my way!
> Can't you see that my burden is heavy?

CLAW

> Surely I'll make way!
> But please tell me,
> where are you taking that stump?

A MAN CARRYING A STUMP

> This is tough heartwood!
> Curled out of a Karelian birch!
> I'll plane a trapezoid of it,
> since the absolute truth lies in there!

CLAW

I, too, believe in nature!
There is nothing in the human being!
O comrade, please tell,
where did you find that!

A M A N   C A R R Y I N G
A S T U M P

It's a secret,
but I am ready to divulge it
for a comrade-in-love!
Follow this road till you see a hazel bush
next to a hole of a badger,
then enter the woods.
Walk a decent distance,
and you'll encounter the Spring of Ideas.
Lilies and spatterdocks dance there!

CLAW

Is it really true
that the Spring of Ideas exists,
although I have believed it fiction?

A   M A N   C A R R Y I N G
          A   S T U M P

True it really is!
Take care, though, since the World of Ideas
is too much for many.
They get lost in its gurgle.

CLAW

I know how to be careful!
Thank you for your advice,
Man with a Stump!
I am off to the spring now,
it is an undefeatable topic!

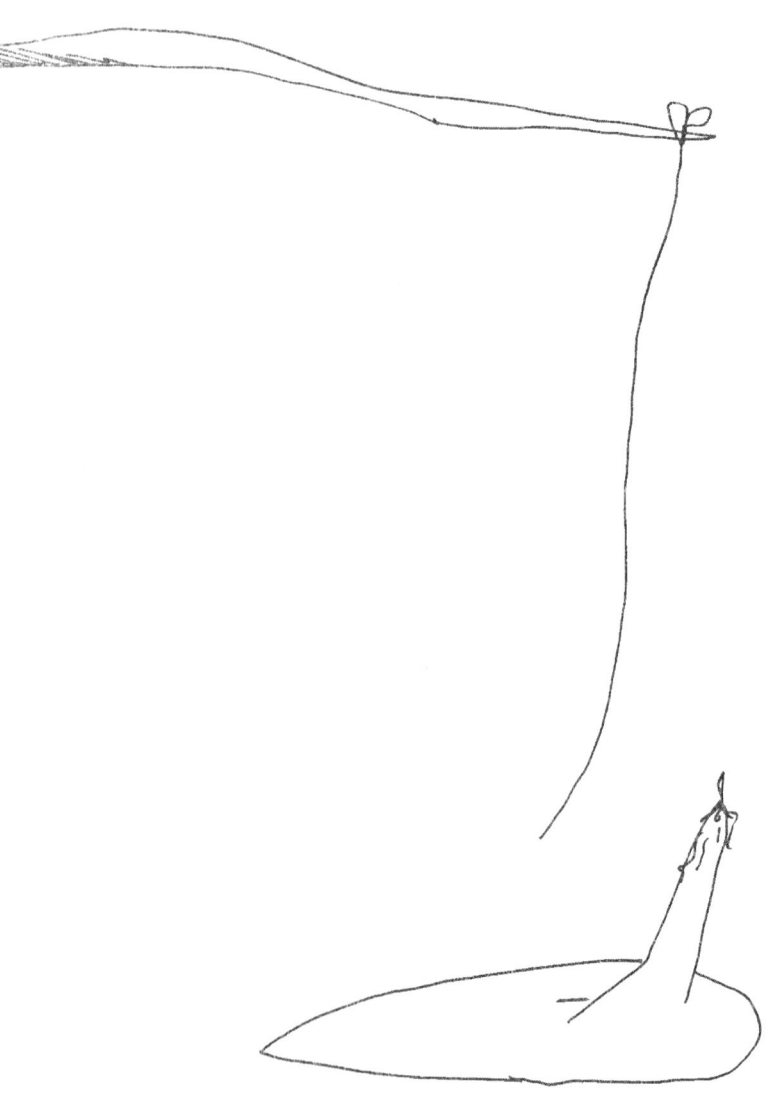

NARRATOR

So Claw took off,
arriving at nightfall.
Tired, he decided to lay down
but he didn't fall asleep directly.
The words of the Messenger of Palorius
kept him awake.
Finally, he fell into a deep, deep sleep.

SCENE SIX

NARRATOR

Claw slept on a moss bed,
when the first ray of dawn woke him up.
He tightened his canvas
and took out his brushes,
starting to work.

C L A W

My linen tautens!
Like a drumhead, it has the right tone!
This landscape! This life!
Whitecaps, whirls, and swells,
let the spring flow into me freely!

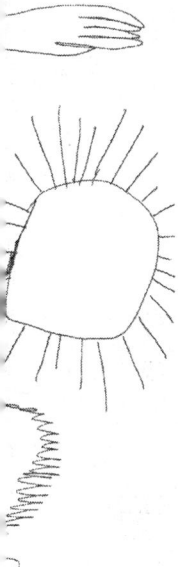

(Claw squeezes paint on canvas.)

C L A W

Like honey out of the tube,
let my colors shine!
Okra and burnt sienna,
sinoper and Napoleonic yellow!
These are the colors of my orchestra,
my brushes be the baton!
I as the conductor à la Toscanini!
The Messenger of Palorius
shall name me master!

NARRATOR

And so Claw painted all morning
and afternoon,
until the day turned to night.
Claw put down the brush
and contemplated the finished painting.
He noticed that he wasn't satisfied
with his work.
Claw decided to end the day's work
and recline on the moss bed.

NARRATOR

It was dark and quiet,
until the Moon protruded
and gleamed its wan light on the spring.
That was the end of quiet:
a faint gurgle began.
It grew louder and louder,
waking Claw up.
He stood and looked at the spring,
noting that the surface of the water
had become a mouth, spitting foam.
Froth and bubbles of phlegm
soon disappearing,
sounds filled the air.

SPRING

L'uomo non è che una canna,
la più fragile di tutta la natura;
ma è una canna pensante.
Non occorre che l'universo
intero si armi per annientarlo:
un vapore, una goccia d'acqua è sufficiente
per ucciderlo.
Ma quand'anche l'universo lo schiacciasse,
l'uomo sarebbe pur sempre
più nobile di chi lo uccide,
dal momento che egli sa di morire
e il vantaggio che l'universo ha su di lui;
l'universo non sa nulla.

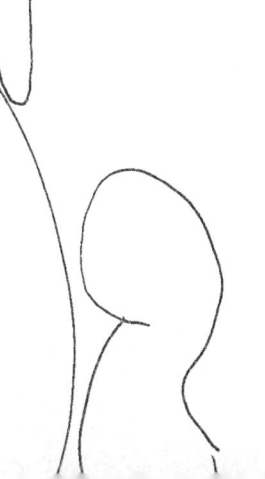

NARRATOR

The spring fell silent,
and the mouth became
the surface of the water once again.
Claw did not comprehend
the language of the spring,
which made him very, very sad.
He dug out a bird whistle
resembling Hannibal the Duck
and blew into it,
but the spring remained mute.

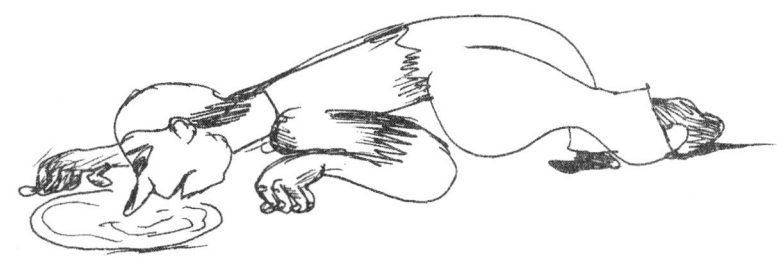

SCENE SEVEN

NARRATOR

The morning began to dawn,
and nature woke up.
Claw packed his stuff
and returned to the road.
But he did not notice
that the constellation of Vicovarius
shone bright in the sky.
The branch of the rowan tree cracked,
the odor of sulfur rose from the ground,
Rick the Rat fled to a hole.
The Messenger of Palorius
had returned.

THE MESSENGER OF PALORIUS

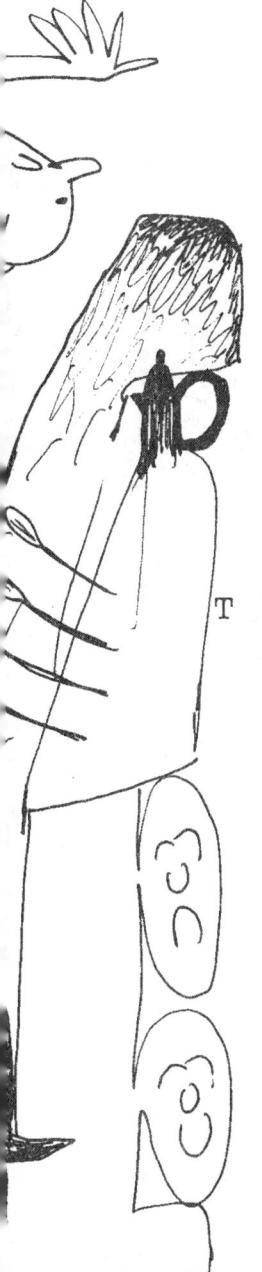

I am the Messenger of Palorius,
I observe the time, see the direction,
and master absolute speed.
I came to see your painting,
as had been settled.

CLAW

You came too soon, O Messenger!
It requires a finishing touch!

THE MESSENGER OF PALORIUS

You failed, as I foretold.
The lilies and spatterdocks
do not dance on the canvas.
The rat has been thrown into the water.

CLAW

Water plants are sure to dance
on my canvas!
The lilies of Monet will look like weeds!
I just need some time,
until they celebrate me as the master.

THE MESSENGER OF PALORIUS

You will experience success
but will not find satisfaction.
Listen, Claw,
I bring you a message
from the centaur of Greatius,
the young sireless.

CLAW

Is it really the noble fatherless
who addresses me?!

THE MESSENGER
OF PALORIUS

This is the message:

The wet fur swims upstream,
the back of the tired one
turns toward the bottom,
phosphorus stars glowing in the eyes.
At that moment, the time is right.

CLAW

I understand the message of the centaur!
One cannot trust nature,
it is lifeless in its soul.
In my own soul I have everything!
I now know what art is,
art is confession!
Hence, I intend to confess!

(The Messenger of Palorius disappears.)

SCENE EIGHT

NARRATOR

Claw decided to settle down
and return to his old home.
There he waged the war of the soul,
preserving his skirmishes on linen.
Paintings there were many,
receiving attention and praise.
Claw was famous throughout the land,
and many admired his torment.
He was called the master, but,
as predicted by the Messenger of Palorius,
this sudden success did not satisfy Claw.

C L A W

Let the whistles of the fowler blow!
What am I?!
Nothing or someone?
Methinks that art in me speaks
but how do I get it out?
The sound of my self,
that struggle of the soul,
may it become colors on the canvas!

I want to be king!
Like a noble pine, rising high,
but is it pus that works inside of me?

Out with you, rats and mice!
It is not the time of victory!

O the ear of Vincent!
What holds my hand back?
My line does not find the soul,
I retreat behind a mask.
When will I exuviate and split my tongue?
O horror, what am I saying?!
Surely I am not a black adder
of the wasteland!

ACT TWO

SCENE ONE

NARRATOR

Michael the Teen
lived in a lovely fishing village
in the river delta.
Though young in age,
he had for a long time dreamed
about becoming an artist,
practicing forms with charcoal,
even painting with egg tempera.
But as his day job
he let the blood of old folks
in the hospice of Tetranius.

MICHAEL THE TEEN

I will bring out your fragile vein!
Ah—this is how we do it!
I can feel the artery!

NARRATOR

This is how Michael spent his time,
fall already advanced,
arrived the first frost,
the wryneck migrated south
from its home,
the beech tree.
This formed a sign for Michael the Teen
to at last go and talk to Claw.

MICHAEL THE TEEN

Enough with the blood-letting!
Cat paws will turn into those of a lion!
I will meet Claw
and shed my last milk tooth!
This is my travel song:

I will light up the candle of art
and carry it in my bosom!
A storm cannot extinguish its flame,
because at its root my soul is!

I am pure and innocent,
hence my art is true!

Blue is the color of the sky,
green the grass, the lawn,
yellow the color of grain,
red is the sun when it sets,
and white—white is all.

Hence I will light the candle of art!

NARRATOR

So left Michael,
carrying his sketchbook.
He needed to get to a ship
and sail across the sea,
but he didn't have a single dime.
When he got to the port,
he sought Captain Odobenus,
the famous half-human,
and put forward a proposal:

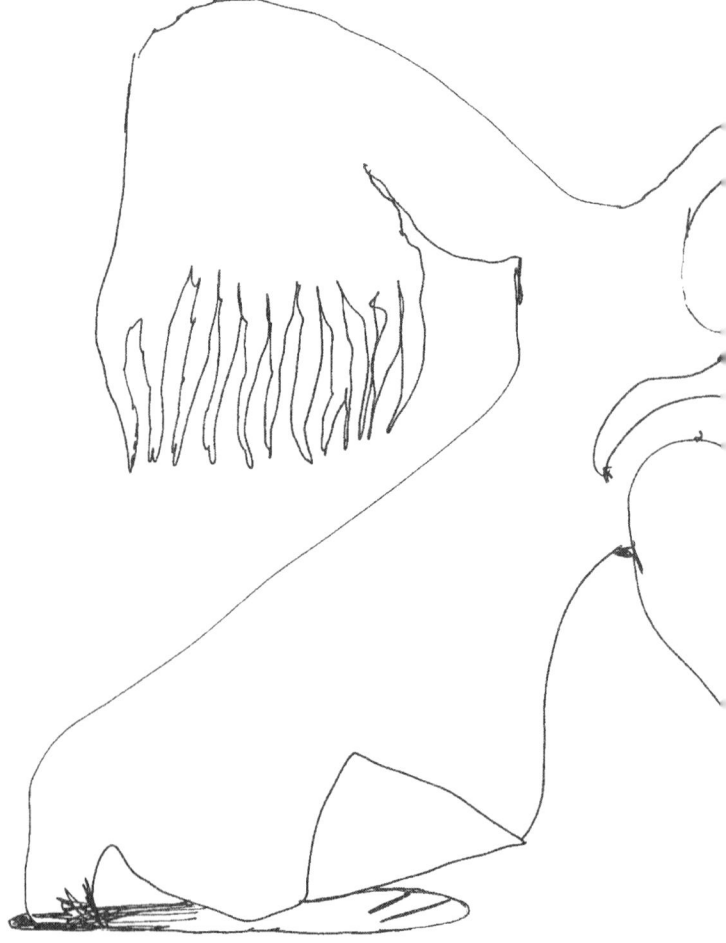

MICHAEL THE TEEN

O splendid sea lion, hear me out!
    Let me board your ship,
and I will commit you to canvas!

CAPTAIN ODOBENUS

Come aboard, lad!
I'm a lover of pictures.
But should you fail,
I will gore you with my tusks!

(Michael the Teen boards the ship.)

MICHAEL THE TEEN

O savage half-human,
know that I cannot fail,
for my soul is innocent.
Already when we were conversing,
I sketched you on my canvas,
and now strokes one, two, and four!
Ah, colors five and six!
A drop of ceruse is the finishing touch!
What do you think about it,
Captain Odobenus?

CAPTAIN ODOBENUS

You highlighted the salt furrows
of my countenance charmingly!
Purple haze rises from my crooked pipe!
My tusks shine like sapphire!
No one else has a similar skill!
Let the foghorns celebrate your success!

SCENE TWO

NARRATOR

Michael the Teen arrived in the harbor
and continued his journey.
He was taken on a carriage,
and soon the city towers loomed before him.
The driver stopped the wagon,
letting the horses rest.
Michael decided to alight
and walk the rest of the way.

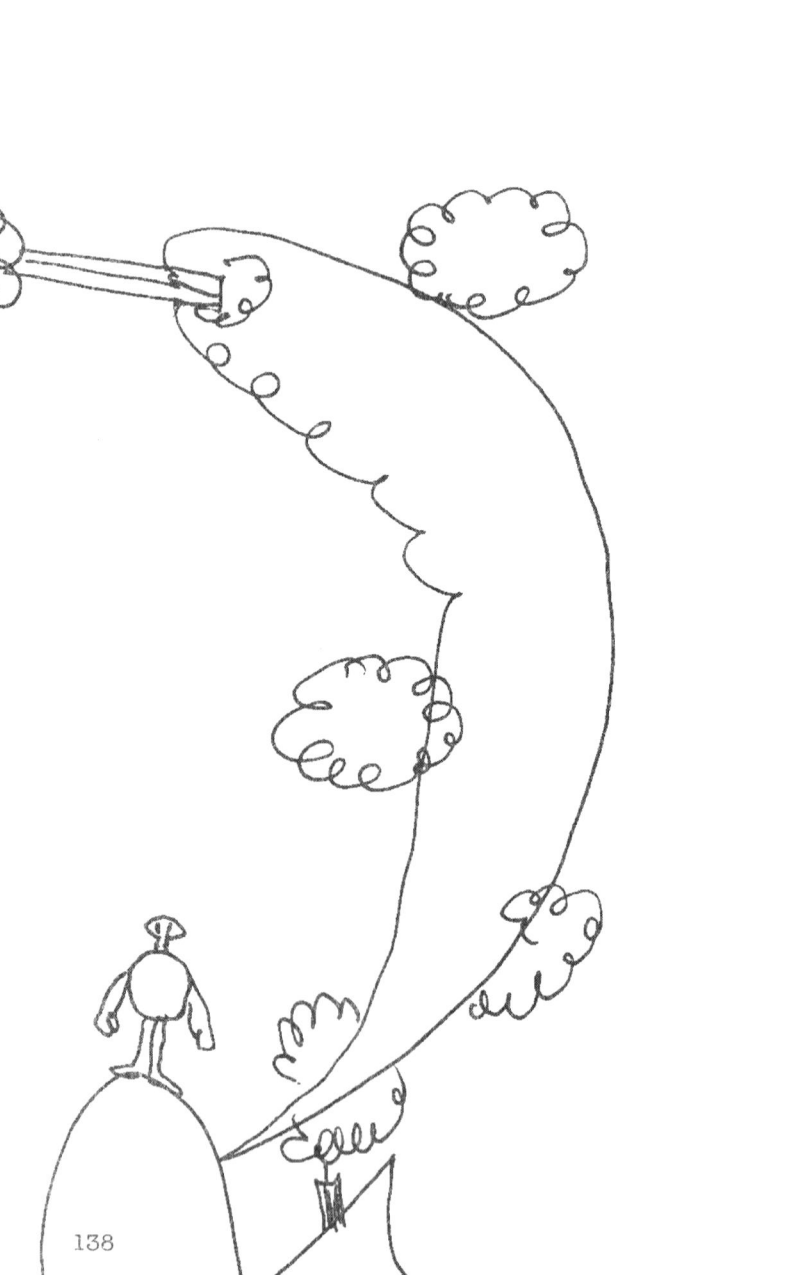

MICHAEL THE TEEN

I've seen those towers only in paintings!
Now they become forms in flesh!
Claw was correct in his Turnerian analysis:
a stroke finds a form,
with a drop of bone white on top of it!

NARRATOR

Now, Michael didn't realize in his ecstasy
that there was another teen
walking by his side,
addressing him:

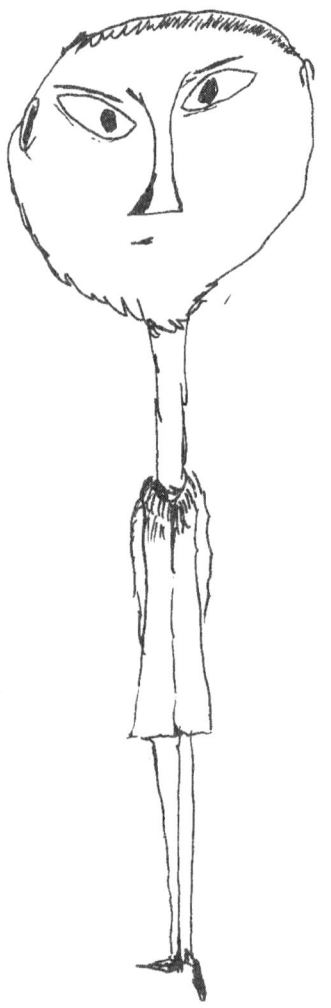

ANOTHER TEEN

Faults reside in your speech!
I, too, am familiar with Claw's analysis,
but I deem it rubbish!

MICHAEL THE TEEN

You utter odd words, stranger.
Has the Worm completed his deeds?

ANOTHER TEEN

I abandoned Claw's way a long time ago.
Art must not be shrouded in wolf skin.
Did I understand right
that you are en route to Claw's?

MICHAEL THE TEEN

Correct, for he carries the cloak of honesty,
paints with the torch of joy and agony!

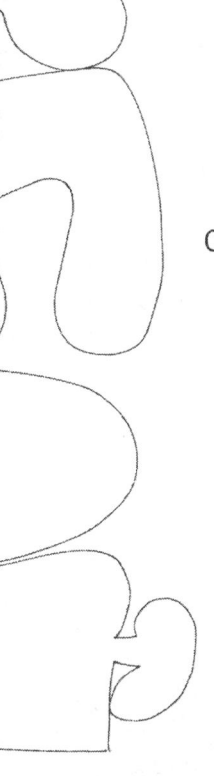

A N O T H E R T E E N

Reconsider what you are embarking upon,
because he leads people with scaly hands,
speaks with a forked tongue,
imprisons people in his twisted mind.
Beware, then, rather than admire him!

M I C H A E L
T H E T E E N

Why do you speak maliciously of him
and plant the seed of doubt?
I don't believe your words!
Indeed, I am going to go meet Claw!

SCENE THREE

NARRATOR

And so Michael the Teen
went through the city gates, resolute,
passing the old oak
and continuing to Claw's house.
He walked through the front yard
to the door and knocked.

           C L A W

Is it pestilence, knocking on my door!?

            M I C H A E L
            T H E   T E E N

               Michael am I,
     and I want to dedicate my life to art!
           I came to seek instruction,
             O master of alla prima!
               I, too, love contours!
           Crimson red is my beloved!

CLAW

Even the poison arrow frog
changes its color!
And the chameleon catches flies!
But do enter, Michael the Teen!

(Michael the Teen enters,
and Claw takes him to his studio.)

CLAW

Look around, teen!
These are paintings from my bygone years.
Every one more beautiful than the other,
but acclaim they didn't receive.
But do you see what's in the middle?

MICHAEL THE TEEN

I see a huge canvas tightened,
with base coat ready on it.

CLAW

You've seen correctly!
I will paint my last confession on it!
It will be pronounced the crown jewel
of my oeuvre,
and they will remember me of it.
But enough of that,
what was it that you came to learn?

(Michael the Teen opens his sketchbook
and shows his works.)

MICHAEL THE TEEN

Here is a cheek of a maiden on a meadow,
a mole adorns her brow!
And here, a six-legged eukaryote:
it is a privet hawk moth!
And what about this rat right here,
gnawing the calf of the malnourished one?!

(Claw interrupts Michael the Teen.)

C L A W

Ah, woe! I see myself in your works.
When I was still seeking as a youth,
my line was frail and faith strong.
You do have skill!

(Michael the Teen continues the display.)

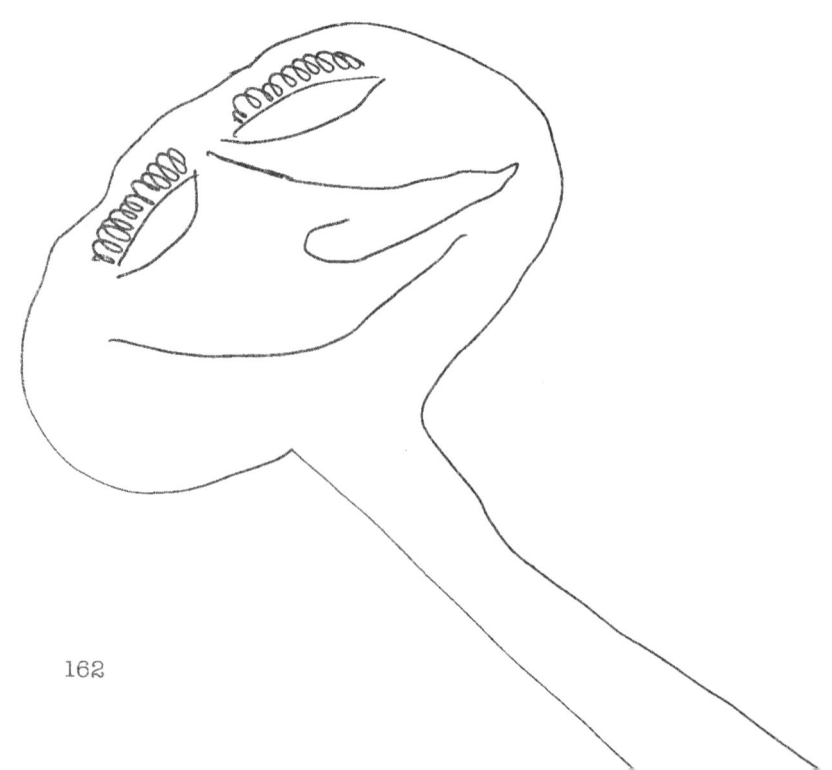

MICHAEL THE TEEN

This I drew in the marketplace,
when they were flushing down
the guts of fish with a water hose,
and here the stepmother is giving little
John a bouquet of lilies-of-the-valley!

(Claw interrupts Michael the Teen once again.)

CLAW

Ah, woe!
I do understand what you're aiming for,
but you have a long road ahead of you!
Your works are lacking spirit!

(Michael the Teen continues the display.)

MICHAEL THE TEEN

But see here the portrait
of the great artist Nerovictus!
I am proud of it!
Truly I captured his soul!

CLAW

You call this stunt a great artist?
He wreaked havoc the day he was born
and the day he died!
And you call that a portrait?
It is a daub of no value!
If you are proud of this,
I will take back my words!
It is futile for you to dream
of becoming an artist!
Get out of my house!

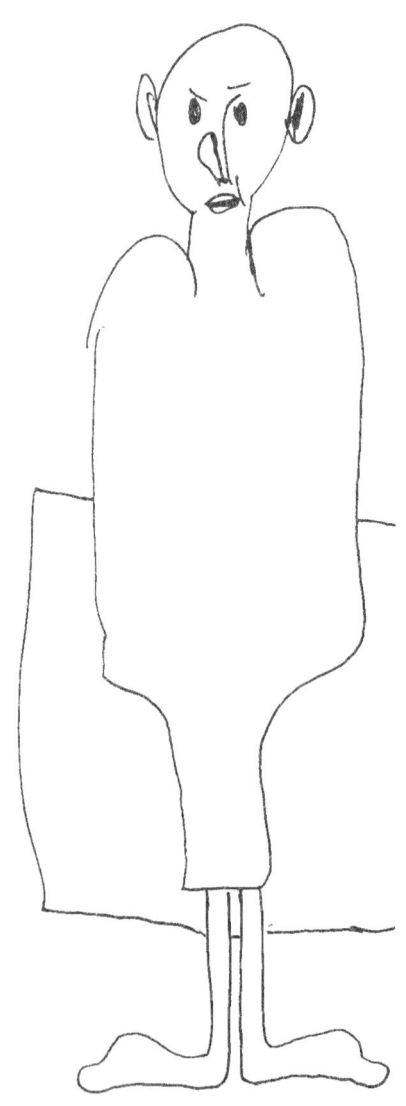

MICHAEL THE TEEN

O master, tell me what I did wrong!
I am ready to learn!

CLAW

I won't take you as my student!
Get out of my house,
you're an affront to art!
Even Lenny the Leech
doesn't want your blood!

SCENE FOUR

NARRATOR

Disappointed, Michael the Teen
walked out of Claw's house
and sat down on the porch stairs.
His mind was in deep contemplation.
He thought long and hard
about Claw's words.

At last the sun set and the night descended.
The Moon protruded
and illuminated the yard.
Then, Michael the Teen jumped
and cried to the stars:

MICHAEL
THE TEEN

I will rise to your height!
The imprint of my work will shine long
and bright!
Now I know what to do,
I will paint Master Claw!

(Michael the Teen dashes in
and finds Claw painting his huge canvas.)

MICHAEL THE TEEN

O master, my master!
Your words certainly true are!
Nerovictus is a coarse fish,
let me paint the true genius!
The soul and spirit reside in you!

CLAW

Get the hell out of here!
Can't you see I'm working?

MICHAEL THE TEEN

O master, my master!
I beg your pardon,
but this is the right moment!
I promise to be quick and,
through my work, reveal your essence!

(Claw puts down his brush.)

CLAW

Poor you!
I will let you try
although I know it to be mistaken,
for your lack of talent
will disgrace my picture.
Promise to leave after your work
and never come back!

(Claw sits on a stool,
and Michael the Teen begins painting.)

MICHAEL THE TEEN

Oh, so was it about this moment
that the buck,
the little faun living in the woods,
sang me fairy tales in childhood?
I will take out my palette and brushes!
I will mix my colors
and not use a thinner at all!

This is the first stroke,
the third and fourth, too!
With these brushes,
I will incite myself into passion,
but my soul is innocent still!
Let the race of ecstasy begin!

O noble master,
now when I paint you
I see you with new eyes!

C L A W

I admire your naive faith.
However,
your skills cannot preserve me in painting!

M I C H A E L
T H E   T E E N

Hold on, you impatient one,
soon I am ready!
The symphony of colors is finalized!
Do you hear the kettledrums thunder,
when my brush belches color?

The contours and forms are set,
ceruse brings harmony!
This is the last touch!

CLAW

So, show me your work,
but brace yourself,
I will not hold back my tongue!

NARRATOR

Michael the Teen showed his painting then,
and Claw took his time observing it.
His form grew dark by the minute,
envy was smoldering in his eyes,
rage distorting his face.
Foam began gushing out from his mouth,
his hands shaking.
His skin became pale,
and blood flew from his gums.
The foam and blood became mixed,
flowing down his chest like rivers.

Michael the Teen
retreated to the corner,
eyes wide with fear,
staring at his master.

Thus spoke Claw:

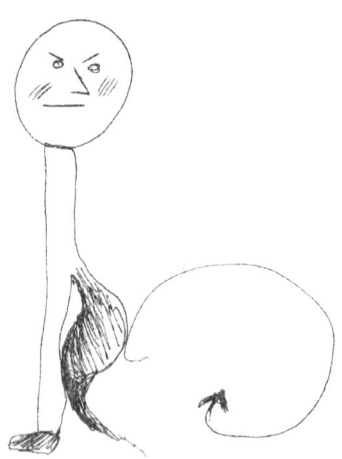

C L A W

You scamp!
May your young spleen rip!
Life might be easy and fun for you,
unaware of the struggle of creation!
Don't you know that evil has wings
and good plods along like a snail?

M I C H A E L
T H E   T E E N

O master, my master, what say you?
I am not evil,
for my soul is pure and innocent.
So let me go!

C L A W

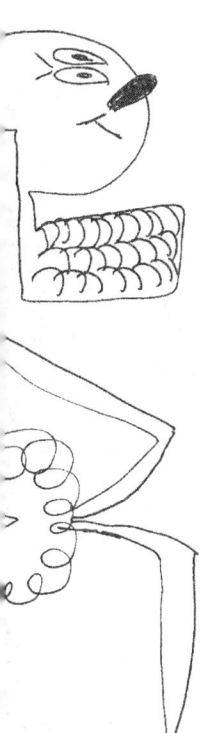

You won't make it out from here!
I will give the wings to the snail!
I need your purity and innocence!
To confess, one must taste blood!
I understand it at last!

I will eat you alive!
I will skin you with my claw,
peck the meat off your bones!
Your liver so tasty,
kidneys the dessert!

This will be my new mixture of paint.
Soon, the blood of the teen will flow!

NARRATOR

Michael the Teen screamed in agony
when Claw sank his sharp teeth
into his flesh.
After eating,
Claw turned to his canvas
and vomited all he had in him.

SCENE FIVE

NARRATOR

Claw fell into a deep delirium,
lying in front of his painting,
unconscious.
The blood dried on the canvas
and a new night fell
before he was revived.
Having risen, Claw noticed
that the Messenger of Palorius
was standing before him.

CLAW

Ah! You, noble Messenger,
have returned to me!
When did you enter my house?

THE   MESSENGER
OF   PALORIUS

I am the Messenger of Palorius,
I observe the time, see the direction,
and master absolute speed.

I have kept watch over your sleep
for many hours,
listening to you talk to yourself,
scrutinizing the rhythm of your breathing.

CLAW

Oh my! So very odd have my dreams been,
I saw phosphorus burn in the bedrock
surrounded by fluorescent ribbons of light,
and on the edge I heard a wheel
that churned glimmering gold,
through which diamonds flew like rivers!

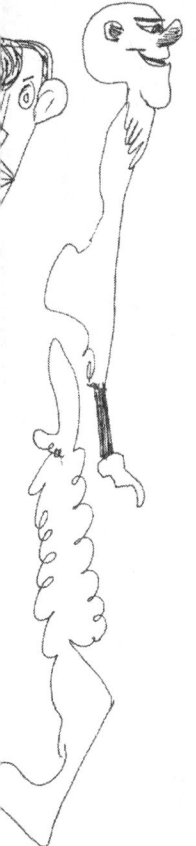

THE MESSENGER
OF PALORIUS

Your dreams were not delirious.
You saw the garden
of the centaur of Greatius,
the young fatherless.
We will soon journey there,
but look at your painting.
What do you see?

C L A W

Ah! It brings out nicely the rusty contours
of my gastric acid.
This work is of utmost purity!

In the past,
I would paint like a cripple in love
running in the meadow,
wobbling amid flowers like a fool
with an erect brush.
The teachings of Sastrapolus
meant the world to me,
but that did not suffice.

I left my crutches at the gates of the
Nerovictus Academy,
not walking with a limp
on the way of art anymore.
I received the leather wings
of a black albatross on my back,
yet in my chest
the heart of a tiny shrike beats.

I flew to the world with wide wings,
I played the part of a giant,
and many mistook me for one,
but my spleen rejected the shrike heart
that I carried.

CLAW

For a long time, I sniffed art around me,
but my sense of smell let me down.
My works couldn't give me satisfaction,
for anosmia plagued my hand.

Now, at last, I apprehend
and acknowledge
that I am no German pointer,
that yellow-haired goliath.
Nor Tritonius the black albatross,
who rules the skies.
My greatest strength
is that tiny shrike
whose neck I tried to break
for a long time!

THE MESSENGER OF PALORIUS

A step toward the stream,
the drowned one does not swim.
The moment of departure is at hand.
Let us toast with the ever-lasting seed
of the horse chestnut that I will squeeze
into a cup in front of you.

C L A W

So shall we do,
and following what Morris the Otter
said on his birthday,
this will be my toast:

See,
for a long time I deemed art the sacred fruit,
using its porous surface
as the mirror of my soul.
But now I understand that one must throw
the common fruit into a basket,
and stamp it with one's feet
until the juice flows,
becoming wine, intoxicating.

Art does not entail greatness,
art does not save the world.
All is play, and all play
eventually comes to an end!

Here's to you, dear observer of time,
marker of direction!

THE MESSENGER OF PALORIUS

The glass of the thirsty one is empty.
The soaked rat swims downstream.
All is play, and all play
eventually comes to an end.

(Claw and the Messenger of Palorius toast one another.)

THE MESSENGER OF PALORIUS

Hop on my back, Claw!
Together we will bend though
the gate of time,
beyond which lies
the garden of the fatherless!

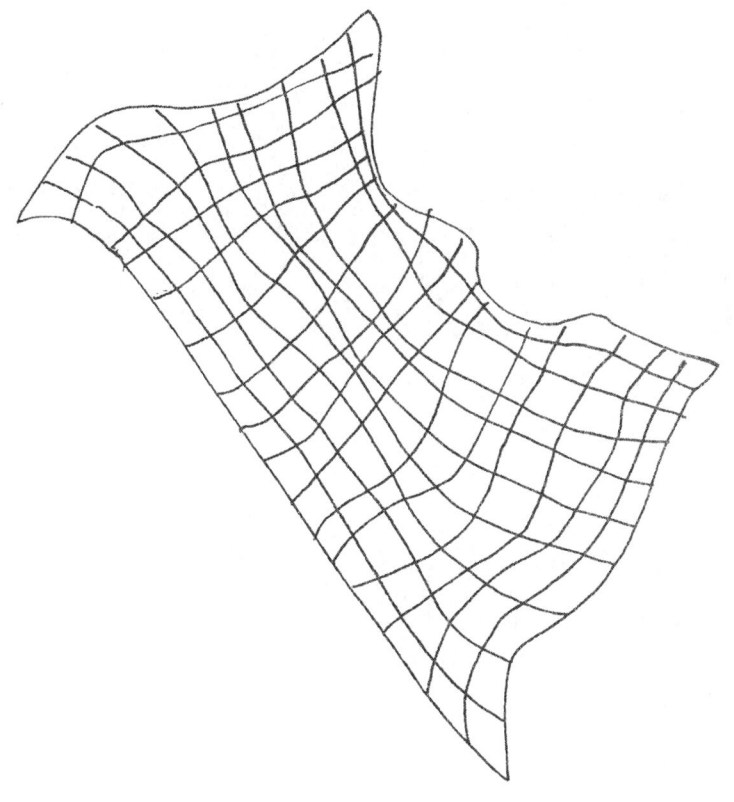